For all the gentle-gardeners and tender-hands nourishing the world.
For the kind-hearted bees and fragrant-flowers beautifying the world.
For the loving-readers and carefree-children nurturing the world.

—H. L.

For Shuzhen Cao—who gave me the whole world of love. I miss you.

—V. Z.

Hunter Liguore

The Whole World
Inside Nan's Soup

Illustrated by Vikki Zhang

"Seeds," said Nanni when I asked her what was inside the big metal pot she was stirring on the stove.

It was the same one handed down from her Nanni. It smelled so good. I couldn't wait to taste it.

"Seeds?" I asked. "How can seeds be inside the pot?"

"Seeds that grew up to be vegetables," Nanni said, smiling. "There are also gardeners in the pot."

"Gardeners, Nanni? How could gardeners be inside the pot?"

"Gardeners, with their gentle hands, planted the seeds that grew up to be vegetables and ended up inside the pot." Nanni winked. "Soil and rain are also in the pot."

"Soil and rain, Nanni?"

"Yes, see them here."
Nanni nodded, stirring.

and then watered by the rain,
before they grew up to be
vegetables and into the pot
for soup."

"In order for the seeds to grow,
they would need to be placed
in the soil by the gardeners,
with their gentle hands,

I stood on my tiptoes
to see.

"We also have the sun, the moon, and the stars inside the pot!"

"The sun, the moon, and the stars, Nanni?" I asked. "How could they possibly be inside the pot?"

"Without the sun, the moon, and the stars, the seeds that were planted in the soil by the gardeners, with their gentle hands, and then watered by the rain, wouldn't grow. So, they are in the pot too."

Nanni put her ear
to the pot.

"Listen, do you hear that?"

"It sounds like a honeybee," I said, listening.

"That's right! The bees pollinate the flowers, that grow up to be vegetables, planted by the gardeners, with their gentle hands. So they are in the pot too!"

Buzz, buzz, buzz!

"Can I see what else is in the pot, Nanni?"

"Oh, yes, there is plenty more." Nanni's eyes widened as she stirred the soup.

"Like the farm workers who pick the vegetables with care. They're smiling as they watch over the fields under the warm sun. They make footprints the rich soil, carrying boxes full of vegetables to t delivery trucks, boats, and trains. And then . . ."

"And then what, Nan?"

"There are delivery drivers eager to take the vegetables from the farm to the market." Nanni smiled.

"I also see the merchants who greet the trucks, boats, and trains. They work in teams to bring the baskets of farm vegetables to the market. People gather curiously to see what they've brought!"

"I guess that's everything, Nanni."

Nanni looked again. "I see a bus!"

"A BUS, Nan! How can there be a bus inside the pot?"

"Not just a bus, but also the bus driver and all the people who joined me on the way to the market and home again."

"Nanni, are there roads in the pot?"

"You bet there are!" Nanni's eyes grew bigger. "Roads and highways—plus traffic lights, bridges and waterways, and all the neighborhoods we passed on the way to the market—and don't forget the electricity that keeps the lights on and the town running!"

"Wow, Nan, I can't believe that's all inside the pot! Anything else?"

Nanni thought some more, smiling bigger than before.

"What, Nanni? What else did you see inside the pot?"

"Love."

"Love is inside the pot, Nanni?"

"That's right. The love of my own Nan, who taught the recipe to my mother, who then taught it to me. One special recipe passed down from generation to generation, beginning with the first Nanni! Just so I could make the soup and share it with you."

"Will you teach me the recipe, Nanni?"

Nanni said, "You'll have to remember everything that's inside the pot. "

"But I already do!"

Nanni looked at me. "What's inside the pot?"

"THE WHOLE WORLD!"

Published by Yeehoo Press
721 W Whittier Blvd, Suite O, La Habra, CA 90631
www.yeehoopress.com

The illustrations for this book were created in watercolor and rendered in Photoshop.
This book was designed by Yanya Mei .

Library of Congress Control Number: 2021930639
ISBN: 978-1-953458-06-3
Printed in China First Edition
1 2 3 4 5 6 7 8 9 10